LOONEY TUNES
BACK IN ACTION™
READER

ISBN 0-439-52140-8

Story adapted by Jackie Glassman

12 11 10 9 8 7 6 5 4 3   3 4 5 6 7 8/0
Printed in the U.S.A.
First printing, October 2003

SCHOLASTIC INC.
New York   Toronto   London   Auckland   Sydney
Mexico City   New Delhi   Hong Kong   Buenos Aires

It was a sad day in Hollywood. Daffy Duck lost a magic diamond on the set of a new spy movie. So the movie director threw him out and slammed the door in his face.

"I'm telling you. I didn't lose it!" shouted Daffy. "A monster took it from me! Take me back now!"

His friend Bugs Bunny tried to help. "What's up, doc?"

"What's up? I'll tell you what's up! I may never work in the movies again, you silly rabbit!" Daffy shouted.

"Don't worry, Daf," said Bugs Bunny. "We will find that diamond."

Meanwhile, inside the evil Acme company, Mr. Chairman was giving a speech. "I've hidden the magic diamond in a very secret place. Soon we will use its power to turn all people into monkeys. Then Acme will take over the world!

"Ha! Ha! Ha! That wacky rabbit and crazy duck think they are going to get the diamond back. It is your job to make sure they don't!" declared Mr. Chairman.

All the monsters, creatures, and aliens clapped and cheered.

Bugs looked at Daffy's movie script. "Hmmm . . . it looks to me like our diamond could be in Las Vegas."

"Um, Bugs, I hate to break this to you, but it's my diamond. You hear me? ALL MINE! MINE MINE MINE!" shouted Daffy.

Bugs turned to leave. "Bye, Daf. Have a nice life."

"WAIT!!! Okay, I take it back," wailed Daffy. "Help me!"

Hollywood

Las
Vegas

Bugs and Daffy walked into Yosemite
Sam's Wooden Nickel Casino.

BLAM BLAM BLAM! A cartoon
cannonball hit Daffy. "Say your prayers,
varmint!" yelled Yosemite Sam.

"Excuse me," said Bugs. "Have you
seen a magic diamond?"

"Sorry," said Yosemite. "No diamond
here."

Bugs Bunny pulled out the movie script again. "It says here we need to go to France, then Africa. But first we get stuck in the desert. Then, I find the diamond, and–"

Daffy stopped him. "But we are partners, remember? What's mine is yours and what's yours is mine. And how are we going to get to France, anyway?"

"Hey, look! I'm a hare-plane!" said Bugs.

But first Bugs and Daffy got stuck in the desert.

"I'm so hot!" cried Daffy. He melted into a puddle.

The Road Runner raced toward them. Then came Wile E. Coyote.

"Beep! Beep!"

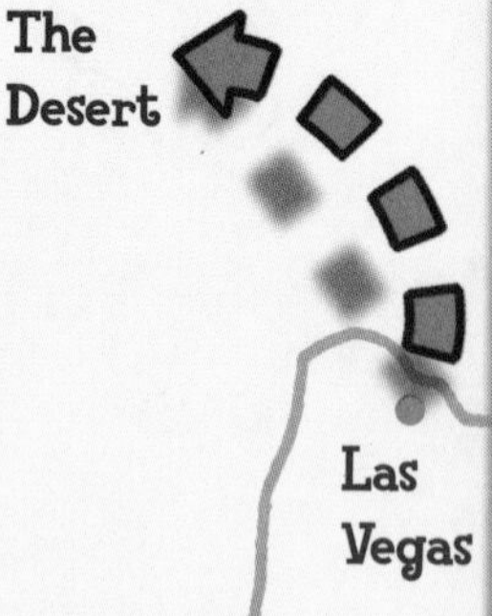
The Desert
Las Vegas

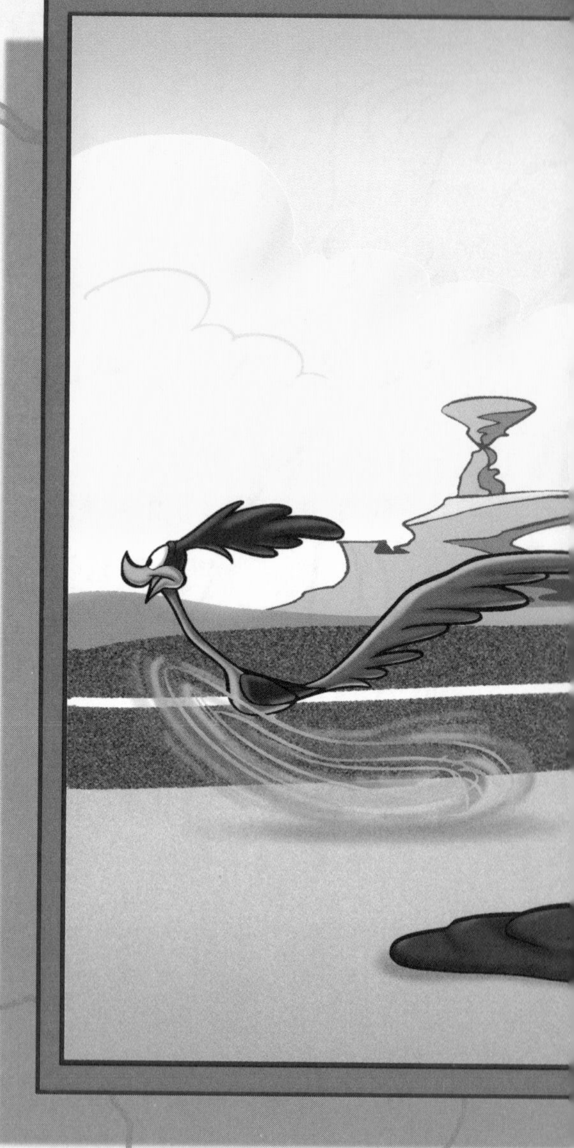

"Have you seen a magic diamond?" Bugs asked Wile E.
Wile E. pointed to a sign that pointed to a gate. The
sign said "Area 52."

Marvin The Martian opened the gate. "Greetings, Earthlings.
I have been expecting you."

"Have you seen a magic diamond?" asked Bugs.

"Just push the red button and the diamond is yours," said Marvin.
Bugs pushed the button.

"No no no no! Not the red one, don't push the red one!!!" yelled
Daffy. A claw came out and stuffed Daffy into a jar.

"Now you've done it, you crazy rabbit!" cried Daffy.
"Oops. Don't worry, Daf. I'll save you!" said Bugs.
Bugs climbed into a spaceship. He flew over Daffy
and grabbed him.

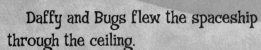

Daffy and Bugs flew the spaceship through the ceiling.

Marvin ran after them. "Stop those Earthlings! Why aren't they eliminated?"

Bugs and Daffy waved. "Good-bye now."

"What's next: a jungle adventure?" asked Daffy. "Dinosaurs? Space chase?"

Bugs pulled out the script. "We're going to Paris, France!"

"*Fantastique!*" said Daffy.

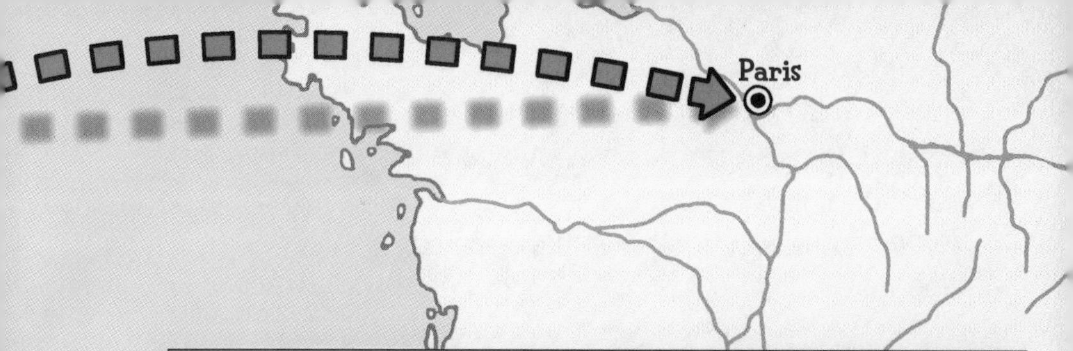
Paris

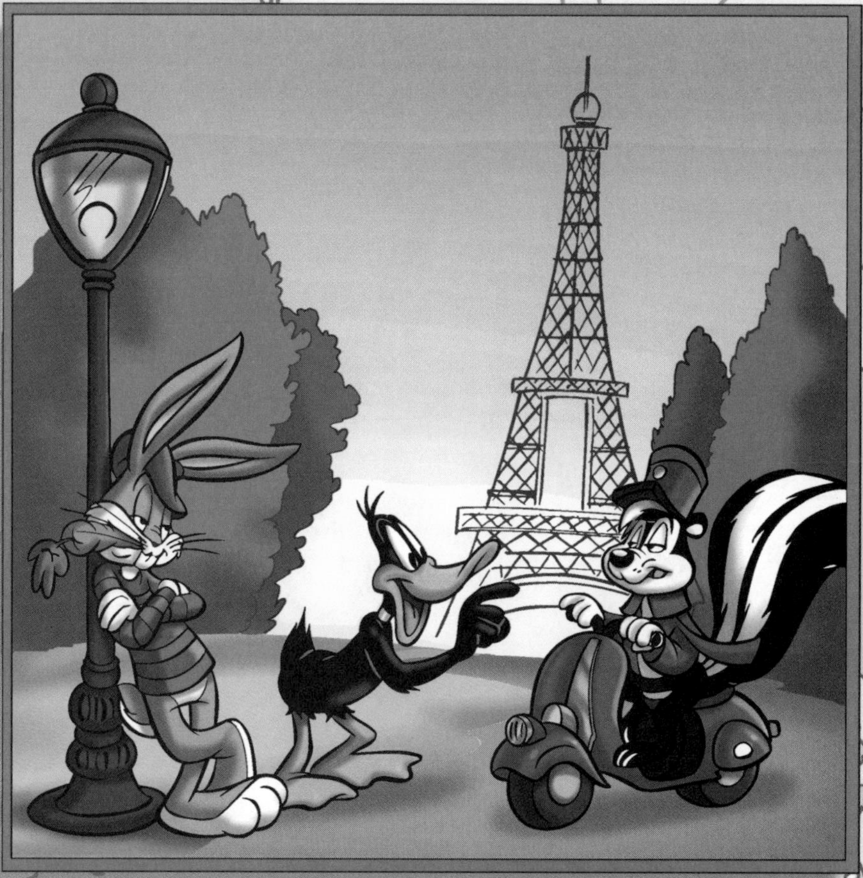

Bugs was enjoying Paris. "Oooh-la-la!"

But all Daffy could think about was the diamond. He waved over a police officer.

Pepé Le Pew pulled up on a scooter. "Police Officer Pepé Le Pew, at your service."

"Have you seen a magic diamond?" asked Daffy.

"Oui! Le diamond is at the art museum!" replied Pepé.

Bugs walked up to the guard at the
museum. "Excuse me, doc. Have you seen a
magic diamond?"

"You know, you look just like a wabbit,"
said Elmer.

"Listen, doc. Now don't spread this around. But I AM A WABBIT!!!" shouted Bugs. "Now tell us where the diamond is."

"You cwazy wabbit! That diamond belongs to Acme! You'll never get it," said Elmer.

"I'm going to blast that wabbit!" cried Elmer. He began to chase after Bugs and Daffy, but they escaped into famous paintings.

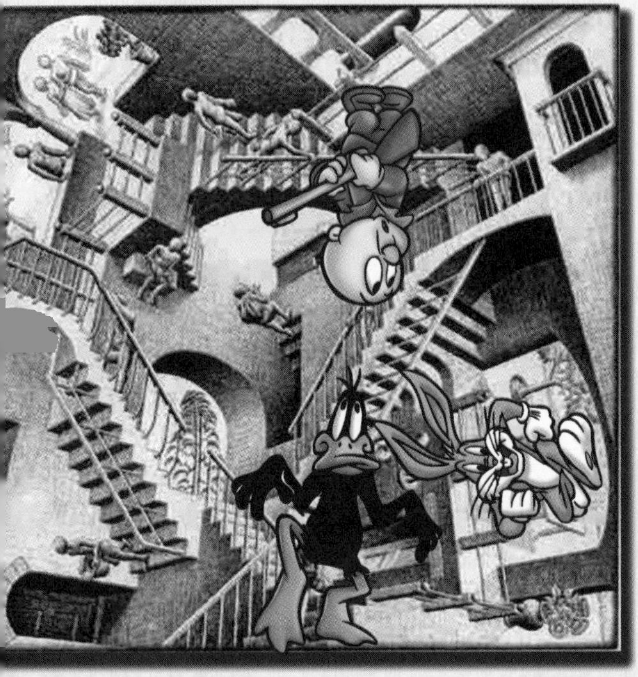

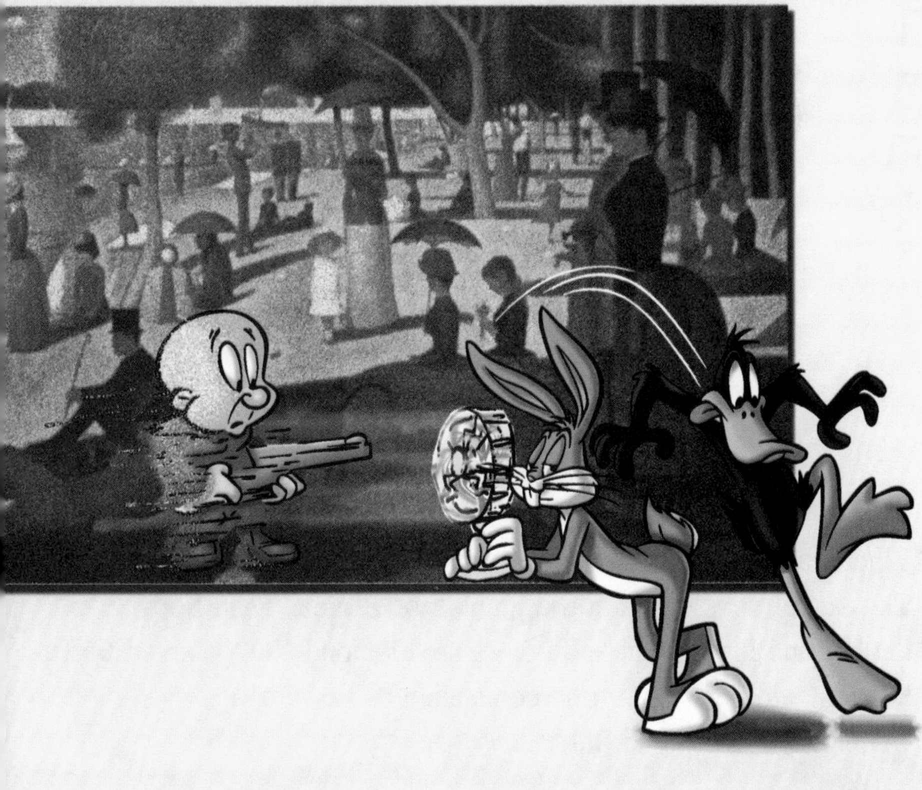

France

Africa

"Where are we now?" cried Daffy.

"The script says we're in the jungles of Africa," read Bugs.

"I'm hot and I'm thirsty and I want my diamond NOW!" cried Daffy.

"All right, all right, quit your complaining!" said Bugs.

"Ouch! My tail!" yelped Daffy.

Suddenly, Granny, Sylvester, and Tweety came by on an elephant.
"What's up, docs?" asked Bugs.
"We're on safari," explained Granny. "Would you like a ride?"
"Have you seen a magic diamond?" asked Daffy.
"I'll show you the way as soon as I eat my dinner!" said Sylvester.
"You bad old puddy tat!" cried Tweety.

"Look!" Bugs pointed at a big stone monkey holding a diamond.
"We are rich! Rich! Let's go!" said Daffy.

But first they had to make their way through a maze of traps. "Ouchy! Ouch! Ouch!" cried Daffy. He set off each trap as he went through. Bugs followed without a scratch.

Daffy was about to grab the diamond when he heard a man's voice. "Take your paws off the diamond!"

They turned around. The evil chairman pulled off a mask of Granny's face. Taz climbed out of a Sylvester costume.

Tweety was shocked. "Hey, you are not Granny and puddy tat!"

Daffy grabbed the diamond and turned to the chairman.
"The diamond is ours and you can't have it!" Suddenly, a
blue light beamed from the diamond to the chairman.

"Look, he's turning into a monkey!" gasped Daffy.
He dropped the diamond.

The diamond rolled over to Taz. He picked it up and pointed it at the chairman. A white beam shot from the stone and turned the chairman back into himself.

"Acme will rule the world!" said the chairman with a mean chuckle.

"Oooh, we were so close to being superrich!" cried Daffy.

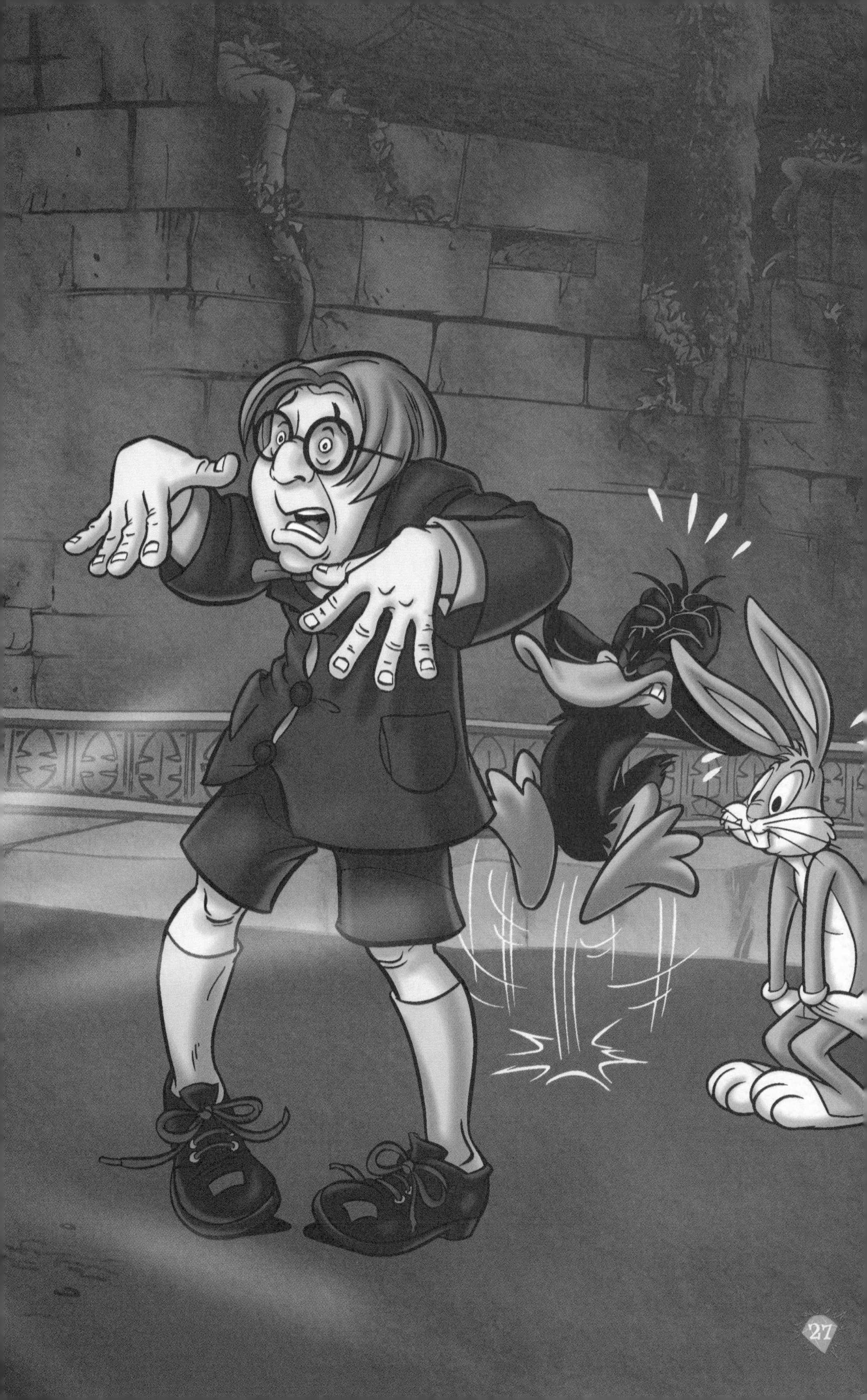

Tweety flew after the chairman and Taz. When the sun hit the diamond, Tweety flew into the glow of the light. She grew and grew and grew until she was a gigantic yellow dinosaur!

Tweety stood in the chairman's path. "You are a very bad man. And I am a very hungry dinosaur." Tweety swallowed the chairman and the diamond in one gulp. Then she spit out the diamond and turned to Taz. Taz was scared. He ran away.

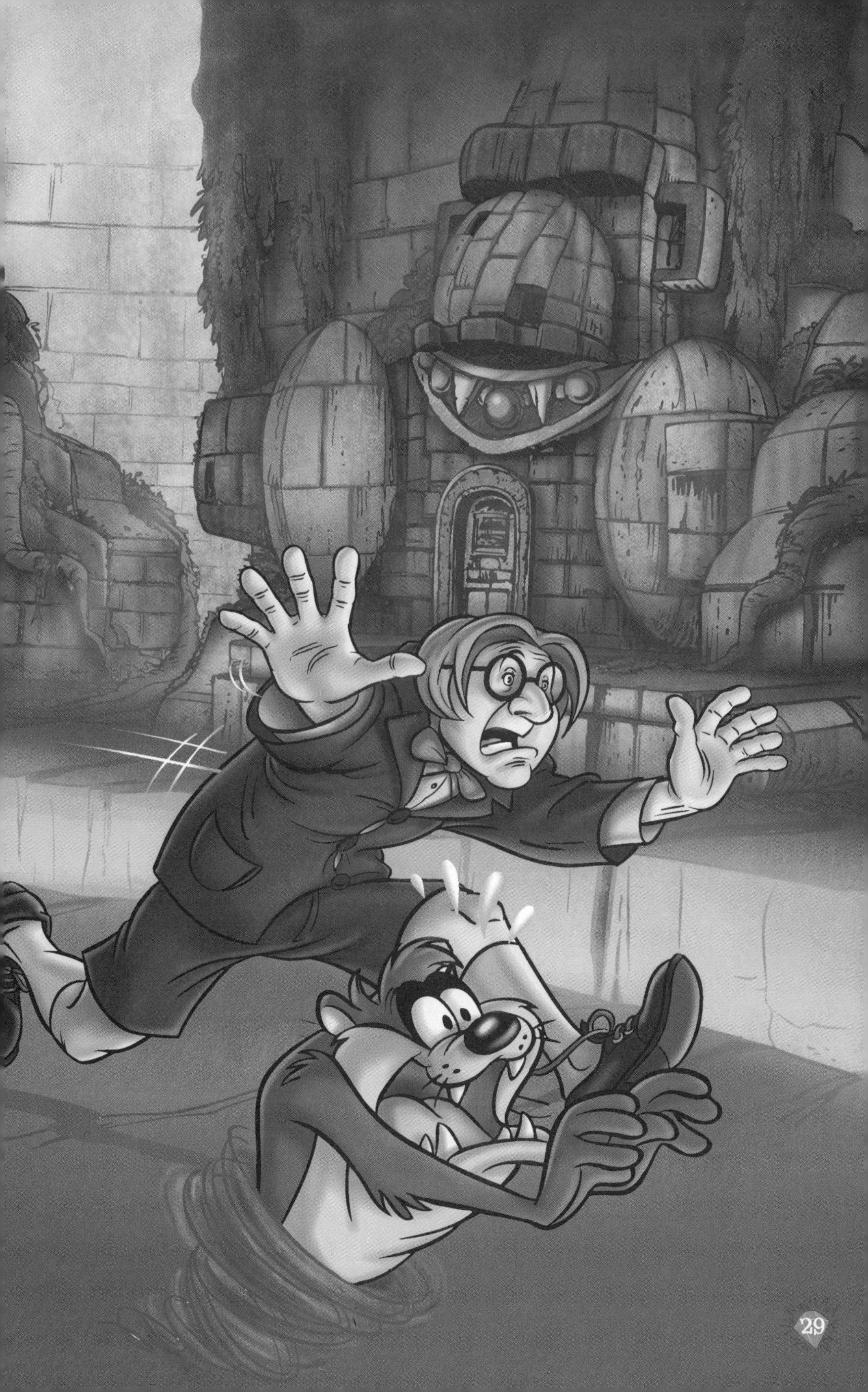

Bugs picked up the diamond and turned Tweety back to her normal size. "My tummy hurts," said Tweety. She burped.

Bugs threw the diamond into a volcano. "Good-bye, evil diamond!"

Daffy cried as he watched the diamond disappear.
"I can't believe we had to throw the diamond in the lava
just because it could turn everyone into monkeys."
"I can't believe Tweety got to be the hero," said Bugs.
"Now you know how I feel!" said Daffy.

Bugs tried to look at the sunny side. "At least you'll get your job back."

"Whoopty-doo," said Daffy.

"That's a wrap!" said Bugs, looking one last time at the script.

"You always get the last word!" cried Daffy.

"No, that would be Porky Pig," said Bugs.

Porky Pig came between the friends: "That's all, folks!"